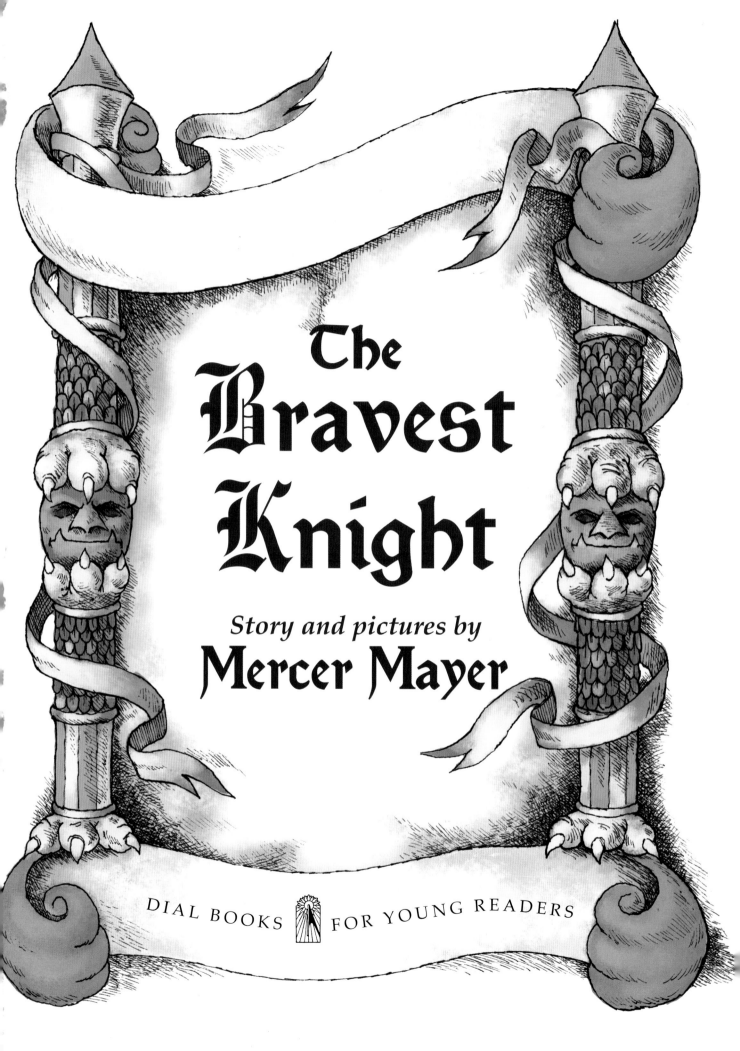

The Bravest Knight

Story and pictures by
Mercer Mayer

DIAL BOOKS FOR YOUNG READERS

DIAL BOOKS FOR YOUNG READERS
A division of Penguin Young Readers Group
Published by The Penguin Group
Penguin Group (USA) Inc., 375 Hudson Street, New York, NY 10014, U.S.A.
Penguin Group (Canada), 90 Eglinton Avenue East, Suite 700, Toronto, Ontario, Canada M4P 2Y3
(a division of Pearson Penguin Canada Inc.)
Penguin Books Ltd, 80 Strand, London WC2R 0RL, England
Penguin Ireland, 25 St. Stephen's Green, Dublin 2, Ireland (a division of Penguin Books Ltd)
Penguin Group (Australia), 250 Camberwell Road, Camberwell, Victoria 3124, Australia
(a division of Pearson Australia Group Pty Ltd)
Penguin Books India Pvt Ltd, 11 Community Centre,
Panchsheel Park, New Delhi - 110 017, India
Penguin Group (NZ), Cnr Airborne and Rosedale Roads,
Albany, Auckland 1310, New Zealand
(a division of Pearson New Zealand Ltd)
Penguin Books (South Africa) (Pty) Ltd, 24 Sturdee Avenue, Rosebank,
Johannesburg 2196, South Africa
Penguin Books Ltd, Registered Offices: 80 Strand, London WC2R 0RL, England
Originally published in 1968 by The Dial Press, Inc., under the title *Terrible Troll*
Copyright © 1968 and 2007 by Mercer Mayer
Text set in Palatino
Manufactured in China on acid-free paper

1 3 5 7 9 10 8 6 4 2

Library of Congress Cataloging-in-Publication Data
Mayer, Mercer, date.
[Terrible troll]
The bravest knight / story and pictures by Mercer Mayer.
p. cm.
Originally published in 1968 by Dial Press under title: Terrible Troll.
Summary: A little boy imagines the adventures he would have if he lived a thousand years ago and was the squire
of a bold knight who fought dragons and trolls.
ISBN-13: 978-0-8037-3206-3
[1. Play—Fiction. 2. Knights and knighthood—Fiction.] I. Title.
PZ7.M462Br 2007
[E]—dc22
2006021321

To my mother and father, my favorite trolls

I wish I lived a thousand years ago.

There would be beautiful castles, kings and queens,
good knights, bad knights, fair ladies in danger,
evil dragons from the mountains, and a giant troll
that roars and eats anything.

I would work for the bravest knight in the
kingdom and be his squire.

I would shine his armor,

sharpen his sword,

and take care of his horse.

I would wear a hat with a fuzzy feather on it and carry a slingshot.

The knight and I would wander
through the countryside in search
of adventure.

We would rescue fair ladies
from bad knights.

We would fight the evil dragon
from the mountains. Sometimes
I would rescue the knight.

And sometimes the knight would rescue me.

We would make the evil dragon
and bad knights pick flowers for
the king and queen.

The king and queen would ask us to save
the kingdom from the terrible giant troll.

We would ride to the giant troll's castle and call
him to come out and fight.

Trolls come out only at
night, so someone would
have to go and get him.
I would guard
the animals.

The battle would last all day.
When night came it would be very quiet.
Finally the winner would come out.

I'm glad I don't live a thousand years ago.